WOULD YOU RATHER?
ANCIENT ROMANS

First published in Great Britain 2023 by Red Shed, part of Farshore

An imprint of HarperCollins*Publishers*
1 London Bridge Street, London SE1 9GF
www.farshore.co.uk

HarperCollins*Publishers*
Macken House, 39/40 Mayor Street Upper,
Dublin 1, D01 C9W8

Written by Clive Gifford
Illustrated by Tim Wesson

ISBN 978 0 00 852180 6

Printed and bound in the UK using 100% Renewable Electricity at CPI Group (UK) Ltd.
001

A CIP catalogue record for this title is available from the British Library.

Stay safe online. Any website addresses listed in this book are correct at the time of going
to print. However, Farshore is not responsible for content hosted by third parties. Please be
aware that online content can be subject to change and websites can contain content that is
unsuitable for children. We advise that all children are supervised when using the internet.

MIX
Paper | Supporting
responsible forestry
FSC™ C007454

This book is produced from independently certified FSC™ paper
to ensure responsible forest management.

For more information visit: www.harpercollins.co.uk/green

CLIVE GIFFORD • TIM WESSON

WOULD YOU RATHER?
ANCIENT ROMANS

RED
SHED

Contents

Introduction

Welcome to the wonderful world of ancient Rome, one of the hugest, most impressive civilizations EVER. It all began over 2,700 years ago and lasted for over a thousand years – good going!

It all started out in sunny Italy, but the Romans travelled far and wide, across Europe, the Middle East and North Africa. They were a brainy bunch who brought the world aqueducts, roads (very straight ones), togas, gladiators and more.

This book is jam-packed with fascinating facts and mind-boggling 'would you rather' questions that will transport you back in time to discover what living in ancient Rome was really like – yes, even the gross bits!

Are you ready?

THE WORLD OF ANCIENT ROME

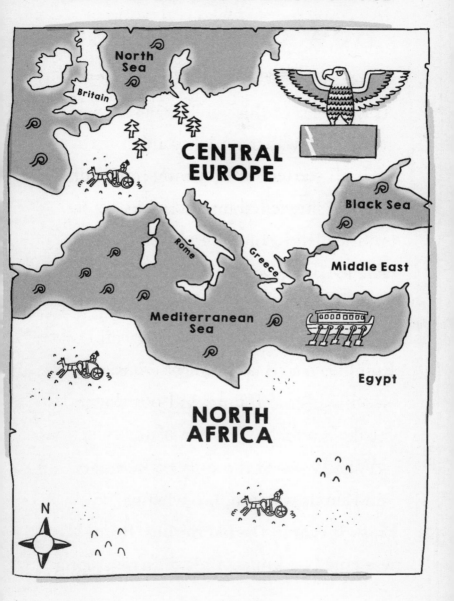

How it all started

At the heart of this giant ancient civilization was the mighty and magnificent city of Rome. According to myth, Rome was founded in 753BCE by twins called Romulus and Remus, who were looked after by a wolf as babies. They managed to survive this unusual upbringing, but all did not end well. Romulus ended up killing Remus and crowning himself king. What a way to get the top job!

Who knows if the story of Romulus and Remus was real, but what we do know is that in the beginning, Rome was ruled by kings. This didn't last long though, as the last one was booted out around 509BCE. The kingdom became a republic, run by people voted in (a bit like democratic governments today, only not many Romans got to vote).

SPOILER ALERT: This didn't last either! After some political trouble and civil wars, the Roman republic came to an end in 27BCE, and was replaced by . . .

. . . The Roman Empire! There was still a government, but it was led by an emperor who got to make all the big decisions. Some emperors listened to the government and what the people wanted. Others didn't – bet they were popular!

Right, now you know the basics, grab your toga, put on your sandals and let's head back in time to find out more . . .

WOULD YOU RATHER

go on a pointless expedition for Emperor Caligula

OR be pranked by Emperor Elagabalus and his many pets?

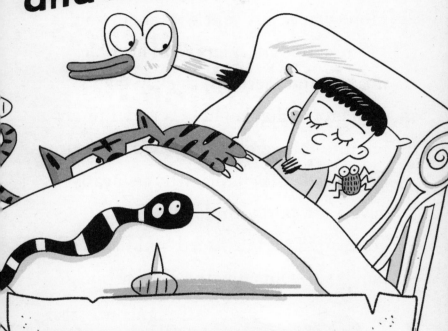

ROMAN EMPERORS WERE A VERY MIXED BAG OF NASTY AND NICE. THE FIRST EMPEROR, AUGUSTUS, HAD A PRETTY GOOD REPUTATION. HE WAS A GOOD LEADER, CREATED PEACE, AND EVEN BROUGHT IN SOME HELPFUL CREWS LIKE A POLICE FORCE AND FIRE BRIGADE. HOWEVER, NOT ALL OF ROME'S EMPERORS WERE SO PUBLIC-SPIRITED ...

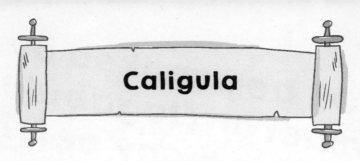

Caligula

Ready for some classic Roman pranking? Hope you've got your wits about you!

Some Roman rulers were horrible hoaxers and merciless mickey-takers. Emperor Caligula (12–41CE) definitely fell into this category. He had a favourite horse, called Incitatus, who he nearly gave an important role in Roman government. He also fed him flakes of pure gold – imagine the glittery poo . . .

Caligula was also a big fan of sending people out on useless, downright silly missions.

Here are a couple of his tricks:

1. He declared war on Poseidon, the god of the ocean, ordering his soldiers to steal shells to teach the sea god a lesson!

2. He sent a messenger on a long trip to deliver a (seemingly) very important letter by hand to another ruler – but it didn't say anything important at all.

These pranks may seem harmless enough, but some of Caligula's schemes were extremely *un*-funny. At one gladiatorial games, he had some of the audience thrown into the arena with wild beasts. Nasty!

Elagabalus

Think you'd rather meet Elagabalus and his furry menagerie? Interesting choice!

Young Elagabalus (204–222CE) became emperor when he was just a teenager. He was a HUGE animal fan, and kept pet lions, bears and leopards in his palaces. He would prank his guests by letting his pampered pets loose during a feast, or sending them into the bedrooms of sleeping guests as a *roar*-ful alarm clock.

Like Caligula, Elagabalus had a very mean streak, too. He once released

hundreds of snakes into an amphitheatre just to see the chaos it caused. Dozens were killed or injured, either by snake bites or in the stampede that resulted.

Bonus fact

Elagabalus may have invented a form of whoopee cushion. Important guests were seated on air-filled cushions which deflated, making a rude noise.

So, how would you rank these pranks? Head to page 68 to meet even more awful emperors.

WOULD YOU RATHER

march into battle as a Roman legionary

OR toil away as a Roman slave?

ROMAN EMPERORS MAY HAVE LIVED IN THE LAP OF LUXURY, EATING FANCY SNACKS AND ORDERING PEOPLE ABOUT, BUT SOME ROMANS WERE NOT SO RICH AND COMFORTABLE. WHETHER IT WAS SCRAPPING WITH ENEMIES ON THE BATTLEFIELD, OR SWEATING IN THE FIELDS, POORER ROMANS HAD IT TOUGH . . .

Legionary

Congratulations, you've joined the finest fighting force in the ancient world!
As a legionary, you'd be a foot soldier, marching alongside your comrades in the Roman army. Let's see if you're suitable:

- AGED 17 OR OVER

- AT LEAST 1.68M TALL

- NOT MARRIED*

- ABLE TO READ, WRITE AND FIGHT!

- PHYSICALLY FIT AND STRONG

- GOOD SIGHT AND HEARING

- ABLE TO SERVE FOR 20-25 YEARS

- GOOD MEMORY (FOR ALL THE COMMANDS AND BATTLE FORMATIONS YOU'LL LEARN)

*If you did have a wife, a speedy divorce would be arranged.

Speaking of good memory, can you remember the whole list from the opposite page? Cover it up quick – no peeking. THAT'S AN ORDER!

The Roman army was HUGE, numbering about 450,000 soldiers when it was at its largest in around 200CE. It was a crack force, and its main mission was expanding ancient Rome into areas with useful natural resources like rivers.

As a new recruit, training was HARD. You'd be sent out at least twice a day on marches and battle drills. Roman soldiers would march 25–35km a day in their leather sandals, carrying their shields and 25kg of other kit on their backs. That's about the weight of a nine-year-old child!

You'd practise day after day how to fight with your *scutum* (shield), *gladius* (sword) and *pilum* (pointed javelin).

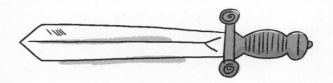

First you'd practise on wooden posts and then other soldiers! (Not with real swords, don't panic – you'd swap them for wooden ones.)

You'd also need to get familiar with some Roman marching commands . . .

PROCEDITE!
(march forwards)

ITER TARDATE!
(slow down)

SINISTRORSUM VERTITE!
(turn left)

GLADOS STRINGITE!
(draw your sword)

DEXTRORSUM VERTITE!
(turn right)

CONSISTITE!
(halt)

All of this training would be watched over by the hawk-like eyes of your centurion, the experienced soldier who led the battalion. Centurions were not a merciful bunch. Mistakes would lead to beatings, no food that day, or worse – a week cleaning out the camp toilets. *Pooh-eee*!

Punishments could be even worse once you were a fully-trained Roman legionary. If you ran away or refused to fight in battle, your cohort (group) of fellow legionaries faced decimation. This meant one in every ten legionaries would be executed. GULP!

But, being a legionary did have some great perks. The pay was good, and it came with a chance to travel the empire, seizing lands far and wide to make Rome as big and impressive as possible – bashing down unruly tribes and rebels who decided to rise up against Rome. There was plenty to be done in peacetime, too. Legionaries might have found themselves building bridges, forts and roads.

Plus, if you survived all those years of battling and building, you would receive rewards from Rome. Most retired soldiers were gifted money and land to build a home on. Result!

Slave

Okay, being a slave might not have been the most comfortable choice. You might have been captured during wartime or born to parents who were slaves. Even if your parents were free people, Roman law allowed them to sell you as a slave. Harsh!

Once sold, you'd have no say about the work you were forced to do. Many slaves laboured really, really hard on farms, in kitchens, mines or on building sites. You'd have no rights, and wouldn't be paid for all your hard work or be able to vote. At least you wouldn't have to worry about getting killed on the battlefield.

Those who were educated or had useful skills might be given nice cushy jobs such as accounting or making jewellery. Others might work as tutors or childminders for wealthy Romans' children.

A select few slaves got really lucky and were set free by their owners – hooray!

Think you'd rather try your hand at some different Roman work? Head to page 32 for some more options.

ROMAN EXTRAS
Eat like a Roman

The Romans had some seriously bizarre ideas about what made a delicious dish. As Roman armies conquered new lands and traders travelled to new places, the range of foods available to wealthy Romans grew. At the empire's peak around 1,900 years ago, all sorts of foods were available – from boiled ostrich to roasted elephant's trunk and leg of giraffe. Here are a few favourite ingredients and recipes . . .

Pig brains

True, some people do eat pork, but the ancient Romans took it one step further and ate pig BRAINS. Yuck! Check out this brainy dish:

TAKE THE PAUNCH (STOMACH) OF A SUCKLING PIG AND FILL IT WITH PIECES OF PORK THAT HAVE BEEN GROUND INTO MINCE. ADD TO THE STUFFING THREE PIGS' BRAINS, WHOLE PEPPERCORNS, GINGER AND RAW EGGS. BOIL IT THEN ROAST IT, COVERING IT IN SALT WATER.

Put you off your lunch? Not surprised. Peacock brains were also considered a lovely, delicate dish!

Flamingo tongues

Other ancient Roman birds weren't off the hook when it came to the kitchen. Flamingos were plentiful in Roman times. The whole bird – wings, long neck and all – was eaten by wealthy Romans as a delicacy, but the biggest treat of all was its wide, flat tongue. We're not 100% certain how it was cooked, but it may have been seared over an open fire or roasted like many other Roman meats.

Stuffed dormice

If you'd rather fly away from flamingo tongue, there was always a cute whole dormouse to dine on. These were very popular with wealthy Romans. Dormice were often fattened up by placing them in a type of storage jar called a *glirarium*. These had air holes, water pots and trays full of seeds, nuts and acorns. The dormice gorged on their grub and packed on the weight – being trapped in the jar meant they couldn't run it off!

Dormice were sometimes stuffed with pork or nuts and herbs, then roasted. Once cooked, they were often drizzled with or dipped in honey, making them a sweet treat . . . if you could stomach it.

He told me to get stuffed. The irony . . .

WOULD YOU RATHER

work as
a poo
collector

OR as a funeral clown?

SOME ROMANS HAD VERY SERIOUS JOBS SUCH AS LORDING IT AS A MIGHTY EMPEROR (SEE PAGE 68) OR WIELDING A HEFTY SPEAR AND GOING INTO BATTLE (SEE PAGE 20). BUT THERE WERE SOME ROMAN OCCUPATIONS THAT WERE A LITTLE MORE UNUSUAL ... OR SHOULD THAT BE UN-*POO*-SUAL ...

Poo collector

This job would make you
one of ancient Rome's true
pooperheroes. A poo collector,
or *stercorarius*, worked door-
to-door performing an
extremely useful (if very
unpleasant) task. Most
Roman homes didn't
have toilets. People
used public loos
when out and
about and kept
their own private
pot for poos at
home. A poo

collector would spend their days wheeling around a wagon for people to empty their poo pots into.

Once the wagon was full, poo collectors would take the waste and make haste out of the city. The destination? The countryside! (Ahh, breathe in that lovely fresh air – oh, wait, you're still dragging around a pile of poo.) Once they were there, farmers would pay for the poo to spread over their fields as fertilizer.

Being a poo collector might sound *bum*-believably horrid – but you'd get to help a whole lot of people. Also, as it was unlikely the whole city would get constipated at the same time, you'd never be out of work! And you'd get used to the smell . . . well, probably.

Funeral clown

Are you great at impressions? Can you make even your most serious friends fall about laughing? Being a funeral clown might be just the thing for you!

Don't worry, you wouldn't have to wear huge shoes – being a funeral clown, or *archimime*, involved following a funeral procession mimicking the dead person. They'd even wear a mask to look even more like them. Spooky!

The aim was to bring a bit of humour to grieving Romans. It might sound ghoulish, but these clowns were sought-after for funerals. An *archimime* would only be hired by wealthier Romans, so the pay was often good, too!

Bonus fact

Most of these funeral clowns were out-of-work actors. The Romans staged many plays, but their actors weren't pampered celebrities. Some emperors even banned actors from mixing with higher levels of Roman society.

Are your skills more suited to a job with a bit more action and adventure? If so, head to page 58!

Gods hall of fame

The Romans had dozens of gods, each with their own specialist subject (they had gods for some strange things, including bees, crossroads and weeding). Romans would pray to the god of whatever they needed help with – either in one of the many temples of ancient Rome, or at shrines kept in the home.

Read on to discover just a few of the biggest, most iconic gods and goddesses from Roman mythology!

Jupiter

As far as the ancient Romans were concerned, Jupiter was the top-dog king of all gods. (The ancient Greeks thought the same, although they called him Zeus instead.) He was the god of thunder and lightning, and according to mythology, he spent quite a lot of time crashing lightning bolts down to Earth to punish humans who deserved it.

In Roman mythology, Jupiter was married to Juno, goddess of light, women and childbirth – but he wasn't very faithful to her, and had multiple children with other goddesses or women who took his fancy. One of these children was the hugely strong, muscly and successful hero, Hercules, most well-known for completing twelve challenging tasks (the labours of Hercules). Capturing the three-headed dog who guarded hell? Easy! Defeating a flock of huge angry birds with poisonous poo? Not a problem!

The Romans built a HUGE temple dedicated to Jupiter on the Capitoline Hill, one of the many hills of Rome. Here, they would sacrifice animals like oxen, lambs and sheep to try and win his favour. *Ewe* had better watch out!

Minerva

There's no two ways about it – Minerva was cool. She was goddess of wisdom, law, crafts, and war strategy, and was often shown hanging out with her favourite animal, the owl. She was tall, strong and usually dressed ready for battle. Watch out!

Minerva had an unusual birth, as Roman god births went. Her mother, Metis, had been swallowed whole by Jupiter – not because he fancied a snack, but because he had heard a prophecy saying that Metis' child (little Minerva) would be more powerful than him. Minerva, however, did not see the whole

being swallowed thing as a problem, and
burst out of Jupiter's head wearing her
best armour and carrying her pointiest
weapons. So there.

Helmet

Spear
(beware
pointy end)

Owl
(symbolising
wisdom)

"Don't mess
with me"
stare

Armour
(for protection)

Sandals (practical AND fashionable)

Diana

Diana was another of ancient Rome's kickass female gods. There was no way she'd be found sitting quietly at home – Diana was champion of hunting and wild animals and was often found frolicking in the forest.

One of the best-known myths of Diana is an encounter she had with a young hunter called Actaeon. Diana was busy enjoying a lovely bath in a forest stream. Actaeon was foolishly not paying attention to where he was

WOOF!

WOOF!

going, and managed to blunder into this peaceful scene. Diana was NOT a fan of being seen by a mortal, much less while she was naked, so she promptly turned him into a stag. Actaeon, confused by his many legs and sprouting antlers, dashed off into the woods – but was soon found by his own pack of hunting dogs. They were THRILLED to find a stag to chase, and gobbled him up. That's what you get for interrupting a goddess!

Vulcan

Vulcan's main thing as a Roman god was FIRE. In ancient Rome, if you needed to get a fire started, keep one burning to cook or make things, or put a fire out, Vulcan was the guy you'd need to pray to. He was even the god of volcanoes, where his name comes from!

With this in mind, it makes sense that he was often shown as a blacksmith,

bonk

forging swords and other tools with a massive hammer. He was the one gods would go to if they needed any fancy kit – for example, Vulcan is said to have crafted Mercury (the god of communication) a special helmet and some flying sandals.

Vulcan had his own special festival, the Volcanalia, where certain Romans would throw little fish into a fire. No one is quite sure why! (Head to page 88 to hear more about some other festivals in the Roman calendar.)

Now you've ventured through Roman mythology and the adventures of the gods, who gets your top prize?

WOULD YOU RATHER

learn to read at regular Roman school

OR learn to fight at gladiator school?

LESS THAN HALF OF ALL ROMAN KIDS WENT TO THE SORT OF SCHOOL YOU MIGHT RECOGNISE. MOST POOR FAMILIES SIMPLY COULDN'T AFFORD THE FEES, AND FEW GIRLS WENT TO SCHOOL AT ALL. BOO! BUT, IF YOU WERE LUCKY ENOUGH TO BE A BOY FROM A WEALTHY FAMILY, AN EDUCATION WAS DEFINITELY ON THE CARDS. AND REMEMBER, THERE WERE OTHER SORTS OF SCHOOLS, WITH MORE FIGHTING THAN WRITING ...

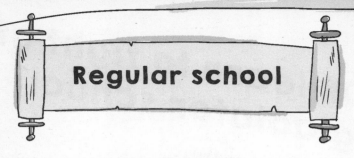

Regular school

Are you a spelling whizz? Know your times tables back to front? Grab your pens, and get ready for a Roman lesson!

A teacher in an academic Roman school was called a *litterator*. Going to one of their lessons would be TIRING – their classes for 6-11 year olds often lasted all day. The *litterator* would teach reading and writing in Latin, the language of ancient Rome. Lots of English words we use today come from the Latin language, like library and umbrella! Simple Roman numbers and maths would also be on

LITTERATOR HAS A SMELLY BOTTOM

the education menu. These numbers
were represented by symbols called
numerals, that are also still used
today. Make sure you're paying
attention – a *litterator* could be
strict. Daydreaming in class or
getting things wrong could result in
a whack or a whipping!

When Roman pupils got to 11
or 12 years old, some moved on to
a *grammaticus*, a more advanced
school where they learned public
speaking, geography and the
works of famous Greek writers
and philosophers like Homer and
Socrates. That would be some
serious *Homer*-work!

MARCUS AURELIUS

Gladiator school

Would you rather do your learning outside, with the sun on your face and the wind in your hair? Well, you're in luck – grab your sword, you've been enrolled at a *ludus* (a gladiator school)!

Actually, you'd maybe not be so lucky . . . gladiators were usually slaves, criminals or enemy soldiers captured in battle, who were trained to become fighters. They'd take part in Roman games held in large arenas in front of bloodthirsty crowds. These were a brutal business – you'd need the training to stand ANY chance of surviving. There were a number of gladiator schools in

Rome training hundreds of new fighters.
And hundreds would be needed – injury
and death were never far away. Gulp.

Life at a gladiator *ludus* would be very
different to regular school. Forget maths,
the only sums you'd be doing would be
calculating survival odds! Training was
tough, and you could NOT expect your
classmates to play by the rules.

You'd be trained by an experienced ex-gladiator called an *ianista* (meaning 'butcher' – not a reassuring nickname). In between all your push-ups and practice fights with wooden swords (still capable of causing a hefty bruise), you'd get lectures on honourable ways to die if you lost a fight in the arena. Gladiators had to stay calm and fearless – no crying or begging for mercy!

You'd learn how to use many different weapons but nothing would prepare you for your first fight in an arena. There, the crowd would be shouting and booing, and you might see a trainee from your school being carried away whole . . .

or in bits. As you saw your opponent approach, you might start thinking, Latin lessons wouldn't be so bad after all . . .

Bonus fact

Gladiator arenas would sometimes have large vats of burning incense, to cover up the smell of spilt blood from previous fights.

Would you be glad to be a gladiator? Or are Roman numerals sounding more appealing? Of course, there were lots of types of Roman gladiator. Head to page 126 for the details!

ROMAN EXTRAS
Top Roman monuments

The ancient Romans were master architects who didn't go halves on their buildings and monuments. Some of them were HUGE. You can still see many of them today – let's take a tour of some of the most impressive ones . . .

1. THE PANTHEON (ROME, ITALY)

This big old temple with a giant dome was built to celebrate a whole bunch of Roman gods. It's still standing today, even though it's almost 2,000 years old. Quality!

2. THE COLOSSEUM (ROME, ITALY)

This mighty gladiator arena
was ancient Rome's
Wembley Stadium (just
more slaying than playing).

3. DIOCLETIAN'S PALACE (SPLIT, CROATIA)

A stunning palace, with 16 towers, fine
statues and giant walls. It was built
next to the Adriatic Sea – Emperor
Diocletian could wave at the waves.

4. BATHS OF TRAJAN (ROME, ITALY)

This MASSIVE leisure complex could
welcome up to 10,000 people a day.
And they all bathed in the nude!

WOULD YOU RATHER

be a rower aboard a Roman ship

OR be a chariot racer?

AS AN ANCIENT ROMAN, YOU WOULDN'T BE SHORT OF BRILLIANT VEHICLES TO TRANSPORT YOU AROUND THE EMPIRE, OR EVEN USE FOR SOME EXCITING COMPETITIONS. IF YOU WERE FEELING *WHEELY* AMBITIOUS, YOU MIGHT TACKLE SOME PRETTY RISKY RACES ...

Rower

Do you like to stay fit? Fancy a life of travel? If so, rowing a mighty Roman ship might be just your thing!

You could see the whole known world as an *oar*-some rower. You might be on a wide-bodied cargo ship, setting sail out of ancient Rome on trading missions to Spain, the Middle East or North Africa to collect goods such as silver, perfume, leather or spices. Or you might end up invading foreign lands in a speedy warship. Some military ships were modelled on a type of ancient Greek vessel called a *trireme*, named because they had three rows of oars on each side ('tri' meaning 'three').

Each oar had to be powered by one or more beefy rowers. They needed to be strong and tireless as they might have been rowing all day. And this wouldn't be some casual paddling – they'd be working every muscle to keep the boat cruising along at around 15–18km/h. Speedy stuff!

Taking a long lunch break or time out wasn't an option (unless you'd managed to sweet-talk the captain of the ship).

Water and ship's biscuits (hard, tasteless crackers) were the main food. As for going to the toilet, you'd have to head to a platform at the back of the ship, stick your rear over the edge and hope for no strong wind (gusts, not farts!).

You would be hoping for a strong breeze when you were tired, though.

As soon as the wind picked up, you could hoist the sails, put down your oars and give your arms a much-needed rest. But don't get too comfortable – you'd still be put to work doing other jobs, such as plugging leaks in the ship's hull (the body of the boat). And those good winds could quickly turn into storms that might sink your ship or smash it onto rocks. Eek!

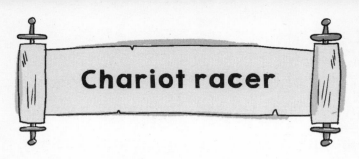

Chariot racer

Are you ready for a *rein*-check? Shout a big YAY (or neigh) and let's get racing!

As a chariot racer, you'd hurtle around an arena called a circus in front of BIG crowds. The Circus Maximus in Rome was 621m long, and could hold almost 200,000 spectators, more than twice the capacity of some large football stadiums!

Where are our seats again?

It wasn't all swanning around in front of adoring fans though. Charioteers would train hard out in the countryside. There, they built their strength and nerve and learned how to handle a lightweight, two-wheeled chariot – either a *biga*, pulled by two powerful horses, or a *quadriga*, powered by four horses.

The chariot itself weighed less than 30kg (about the weight of a labrador dog), with just a tiny little wooden platform to stand on as the much, much heavier horses gave it everything they had. Racing was quite a balancing act!

Top Roman chariot racers were the Formula One or NASCAR superstars of their day. They would race for one of four colour-coded teams: the reds,

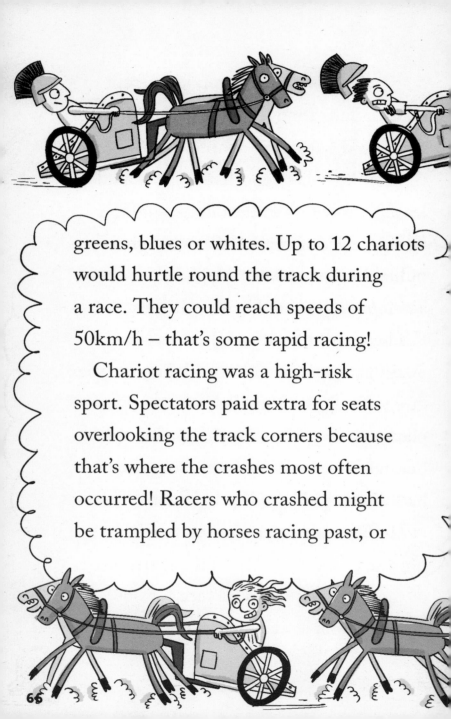

greens, blues or whites. Up to 12 chariots would hurtle round the track during a race. They could reach speeds of 50km/h – that's some rapid racing!

Chariot racing was a high-risk sport. Spectators paid extra for seats overlooking the track corners because that's where the crashes most often occurred! Racers who crashed might be trampled by horses racing past, or

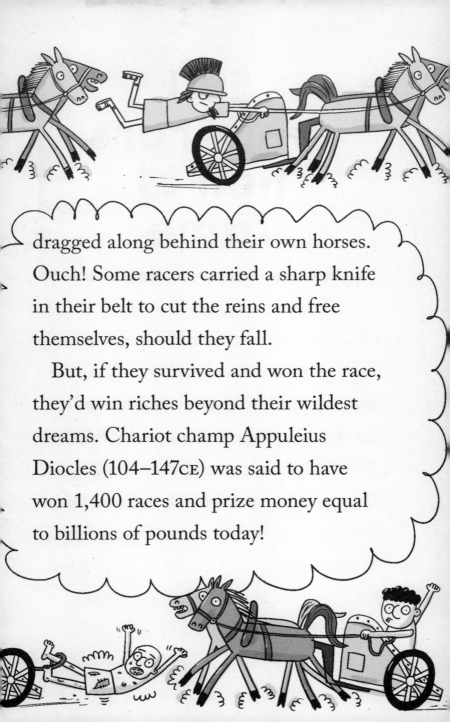

dragged along behind their own horses. Ouch! Some racers carried a sharp knife in their belt to cut the reins and free themselves, should they fall.

But, if they survived and won the race, they'd win riches beyond their wildest dreams. Chariot champ Appuleius Diocles (104–147ce) was said to have won 1,400 races and prize money equal to billions of pounds today!

Evil emperors hall of fame

Welcome to the ancient Roman hall of fame – for the most dastardly, devilish and despicable emperors that ever ruled the land! Roman emperors reigned from 27BCE until the fall of Rome in 476CE. Many of these powerful men used their power and influence to make more lowly Romans' lives HELL. Read on to find out more – and decide who gets your prize for most evil of them all . . .

Violent Valentinian

321-375CE

Valentinian I rose up the ranks of the Roman army and was crowned emperor in 364CE. To his credit, he did set up schools and doctors for the poor in Rome – but that's about as good as it got. Valentinian became infamous for his severe temper. He would explode with anger over the smallest thing and thought nothing of having servants executed for the most trivial mistakes.

Valentinian was also said to have kept two hungry, wild bears in a large iron cage, taking them with him everywhere he travelled. People who annoyed

Valentinian were thrown into the cage,
where the bears would promptly devour
them. Un-*bear*-lievable!

And to keep everyone even more
terrified and on their toes, Valentinian
left the bones of the servants and
advisors the bears had eaten strewn
around his palaces. Not nice.

Septimus Severus
145-211CE

Septimus Severus was born in the north
African city of Lepcis Magna and seized
the job of emperor in 193CE. As one of
his first moves as emperor, he disbanded
the Praetorian Guard – a crack team
of elite soldiers who acted as the
emperor's personal bodyguards. True,
the Praetorian Guard had recently
assassinated another emperor . . .
But not only did Septimus send
them packing, he

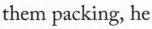

banished them from Rome completely, banning them from coming within 160km of the city. *Guard* luck!

Septimus was a harsh ruler who wasn't bothered about fair trials. In 197CE, he had 29 of Rome's senators executed without a trial or the chance to say sorry. In the same year, Septimus defeated and killed his rival for power, Clodius Albinus – but he wasn't content with just this. He ordered Albinus' dead body to be stripped of its clothes and lain on the ground so that he could trample over it on his horse. He then had Clodius' head chopped off and sent back to Rome as a warning to rivals not to mess with him. Nasty!

Dastardly Domitian

51-96CE

Emperor Domitian was a plotter and rotter – and a vain one at that. Though he went bald young, he had many statues of himself built with luscious locks, and insisted everyone call him, "Lord and God". It was said that he enjoyed stabbing flies with his pen and tearing their wings off. People who dealt with him often suffered just as horribly.

Domitian terrorised servants and had friends and advisors executed if they said anything he didn't like. He had female

Here comes Domitian, better buzz off!

priests buried alive and banished all philosophers from Rome. He also banned any Roman from performing mimes – they must have made a bad impression . . .

All in all, he was not a popular ruler (shocker). He was killed by a group of his own servants who all stabbed him, one by one. No one seemed to mind. His name was erased from Rome's buildings and the senate calmly replaced him, confident that no one could be much worse!

Calamitous Commodus

161-192CE

Commodus' father, Marcus Aurelius, was a respected emperor, who created a peaceful time for Rome – but, sadly, he did not pass his leadership skills on to his son. Commodus left all the empire

ruling to his advisors and instead, spent much of his time wandering about being mean, killing wild animals and servants who annoyed him. *Commo*-disgraceful!

Commodus also took part in gladiatorial games, pretending to be the mythological hero Hercules. He fought in rigged battles against injured gladiators who were armed with blunt or wooden swords, or sometimes not even armed at all, giving Commodus an easy win. He'd also charge Rome one million sesterces (a massive sum of money) for each appearance he made. Cheeky!

Bet you're glad you never met any of these Roman rulers! Who do you think was the most evil emperor?

ROMAN EXTRAS
The good guys

Phew – that was a lot of evil emperors.
Thankfully, it wasn't ALL bad. There
were some Roman rulers who spared the
odd thought for the everyday citizen, and
put some effort into making their lives
a bit more peaceful and enjoyable.

Augustus (63BCE-14CE)
Augustus was called Gaius Octavius
before he became Rome's first emperor.
He created peace and stability, helped the
economy boom, and improved Roman
police forces and fire brigades.

Trajan (53-117CE)

This powerful emperor built a giant market, a forum and public baths in Rome. Good job, Trajan!

Vespasian (9-79CE)

Vespasian brought peace after a time of civil war. He encouraged artists and writers, and championed impressive building projects like the Colosseum.

Hadrian (76-138CE)

This emperor was a soldier who ordered Hadrian's Wall to be built in northern England – a structure to give protection against the prickly Picts who lived in Scotland. He also had a creative soul and spent a lot of time writing poetry.

WOULD YOU RATHER

carry around your boss all day

OR taste their food to check for poison?

BEING A ROMAN SLAVE WAS A TOUGH GIG. YOU WOULD BE THE PROPERTY OF YOUR MASTER, WHO WOULD OFTEN HAVE YOU DO SOME DISTINCTLY UN-FUN TASKS. OH, AND YOU WOULDN'T GET PAID. BUT, SOME SLAVES WOULD GET AN INTERESTING VIEW INTO THE LIFE OF THE ROMAN ELITE FROM RIGHT UP CLOSE . . .

Carry your boss

Are you super-strong? Not bothered by walking through the odd muddy puddle? Why not help your master by carrying them through the streets of Rome?

Understandably, wealthy Roman women and men preferred not to trudge through the grubby city streets. Why get your sandals dirty when you could be carried around? The fashionable ride of choice was a comfy couch called a *lectica*,

carried high above the ground by a group of around 4–8 slaves, called *lecticarii*. The Roman in the *lectica* could watch the world go by, or just have a snooze.

You'd have needed strength and stamina to be a litter-bearer. The *lectica* itself could weigh as much as a person before anyone even sat on it. You'd have to carry your VIP (very important passenger) along bumpy streets, working together with the other *lecticarii* to make sure there were no accidents. One slip or stumble and the whole litter could crash!

Taste their food

Do you think that a life lugging rich Romans about sounds a bit too much like hard work? Prefer to stay out of the hot sun? You could always give food tasting a try . . .

Wealthy Romans couldn't get enough of their exotic grub (see page 28). But, it wasn't without risk. Some powerful Romans took precautions before they tucked into their flamingo starter or their roasted dolphin dish of the day.

Why? Well, at times, poisoning was rife in Rome. It was a favourite way for rivals to kill their enemies and opponents, clearing the way for

their own rise to power. Mwahaha!
Historians think that Emperor Nero
poisoned his half-brother, Britannicus.
And it ran in the family – Nero's mum,
Julia Agrippina, may have poisoned her
second husband.

Poisons were mixed in with food or
sprinkled into a drink. They were mostly
made from plants, such as hemlock,
mandrake, deadly nightshade and the
European yew tree.

To avoid falling foul of these perilous poisons, many top Romans employed a *praegustator* (a food and drink taster). This person would stand next to their employer at mealtimes and take the first nibble of every dish to check it wasn't laced with anything lethal.

On the plus side, a *praegustator* would get to sample their share of fabulous dishes that slaves or poor servants could never, ever afford to buy! Food tasters may even have stayed alive and healthy for years.

On the negative side, the poison in food or drink

could sometimes be
so powerful that a tiny
nibble or small slurp
might be enough to make
the food taster ill, or even
cause death. And you'd have to
try every morsel your boss wanted to
eat, whether you were peckish or not!

Are your taste buds tingling?
Do you like to sprinkle a bit
of sauce on your dinner?
Head to page 104 for some
Roman condiments . . .

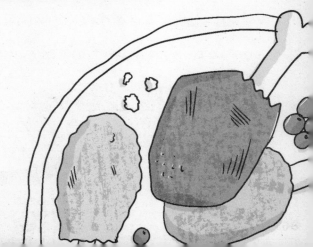

ROMAN EXTRAS
Festivals and frivolity

Being a Roman was often a serious business (especially if you were an emperor – see pages 68–79 for more), but they did love a party. The Roman year was packed with festivals and fun. Here are four events for your calendar . . .

1. SATURNALIA (HELD IN DECEMBER)

Held to honour the god Saturn, this was a public feast where masters had to serve their slaves for a day. Most rich Romans, unsurprisingly, weren't big fans!

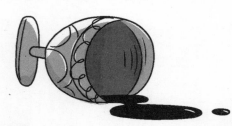

2. LUPERCALIA (HELD IN FEBRUARY)

You'd need to be careful where you stood at this festival. Young men would run through the streets whipping bystanders with goatskin leather strips. Ouch!

3. FORS FORTUNA (HELD IN JUNE)

Good luck today – literally! Fortuna was the Roman goddess of luck. Some Romans celebrated by rowing down the Tiber river on boats loaded up with flowers and wine.

4. ANGERONALIA (HELD IN DECEMBER)

At this festival, priests made sacrifices to Angeronia, the goddess of secrecy and silence. Shhh – you didn't hear it here!

WOULD YOU RATHER

have a poo in front of a crowd

OR take a trip to a Roman dentist?

ROMAN LIFE WAS FULL OF POLITICS, WAR, INTRIGUE AND DRAMA, WITH BIG CHARACTERS TAKING CENTRE STAGE. BUT EVEN EMPERORS SOMETIMES NEED A POO, AND LESS POWERFUL ROMANS HAD TO TACKLE A WHOLE HOST OF EVERYDAY SITUATIONS THAT COULD BE QUITE TRICKY ...

Have a poo

We all know that feeling – you're out and about and suddenly you're hit by a desperate need for a POO. Yikes!

Happily, nowadays there is usually a handy bathroom with a lovely lockable door not too far away to dash into. But things would have been a little different in Roman times . . .

Many Roman homes didn't have a loo at all, so when a Roman needed to relieve themselves, they'd either poo in a pot and wait for a poo collector to come past (see page 34), or they'd visit a public toilet, called a *foricae*.

And public they were! The idea of separate, lockable cubicles had not crossed Roman minds.

In the *foricae*, you'd sit on a long stone bench which contained a row of holes – one for each bottom – alongside lots of other Romans also needing to relieve themselves. GROSS! The wee and poo would drop down into a trough below that had water running along it to carry the waste away.

Sound awkward? It gets worse. For all their achievements, the Romans were missing one thing we now think of as crucial to our daily lives . . .

Fire in the hoooole!

. . . toilet paper!

Instead of this handy wiping method, most Roman public toilets were equipped with a *tersorium*. This was a sea sponge that had been plucked from the ocean and tied to a wooden rod.

These sponges would be kept in the *foricae* in a jug or bucket containing salt water or vinegar. Their business done, ancient Romans would wipe their bottoms with the sponge, then place it back into its container . . . FOR THE NEXT PERSON TO USE. Yes, the sponge was shared, and one sponge might get up close and personal with hundreds of Roman bums during its working life.

If you think that's bad, some less

luxurious public toilets didn't even include the sponge. Instead, people had to wipe themselves using seashells or broken shards of pottery – both of which could be a little too sharp for many Romans' liking.

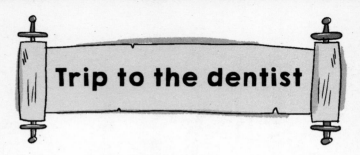

Trip to the dentist

Can you open really, really wide? Are you a champion brusher and flosser? Let's take a visit to the ancient Roman dentist for a checkup!

The ancient Romans didn't have the minty-fresh toothpaste tubes we have today, but their teeth weren't that bad as they didn't really eat much sugar. Though their teeth may not have been riddled with holes, some Romans suffered from worn-out gnashers. They ate lots of coarse, gritty grains that acted like a scouring pad on their teeth. Not comfortable!

Having a toothache in ancient Rome wouldn't have been pleasant – but a visit to a Roman dentist could be even more painful. Roman physicians who treated teeth or took them out tended to be far from gentle, using hand drills, hammers and small chisels in people's mouths – gruesome!

Some tooth-treaters who believed that diseased gums were the problem would sear the gum with a red-hot iron tool and pour honey on the burnt gum afterwards. Agony! And there were no anaesthetics to make your mouth and teeth feel numb first. The most Romans could hope for was a jug of wine before the procedure to dull the pain. With those sorts of brutal treatments, it's no surprise that many Romans stayed at home, trying to painfully grin and bear it.

Some Romans developed some unusual (and probably not very effective) home remedies for toothaches. Roman writer Pliny the Elder suggested finding a frog in the light of a full moon, spitting in its mouth, then asking it to take away your toothache. *Toad*ally effective . . .

Other Romans used mouthwash to keep tooth problems at bay. What do you think was a key mouthwash ingredient?

A) GRAPE JUICE
B) MINT LEAVES
C) WEE

If you answered c, you're right! The
Romans swore by wee, both human and
animal, to gargle with. They thought it
helped whiten teeth and keep tooth and
gum diseases away.

Whilst there is a chemical called
ammonia in wee that may have helped
whiten teeth, scientists aren't sure it was
very useful. It may have even weakened
teeth – plus, it would have tasted GROSS!

**So, will you be braving the
public toilets for an un-*poo*-sual
bathroom experience? Or do
you think you'd rather face
the dentist?**

ROMAN EXTRAS
Roman remedies

Welcome to the Roman doctor's surgery!
Today, you're the doctor, with a busy
queue of patients waiting outside. Let's
take a look at some popular cures for
diseases and maladies in ancient Rome . . .

Cure for acne

Roman remedies were a mixture of trial
and error – a lot of error. Physicians
suggested all sorts of cures for common
health problems, such as acne. One
of their favourites for this particular
problem was placing crocodile meat
onto the face!

Cure for a headache

Dip a chameleon into a cup of wine and then drink the wine.

Cure for nosebleeds and stomach pain

Eat snails! This cure came from the famous Roman writer, Pliny – he was convinced that this slimy solution was foolproof, for both problems. Did it work? Probably not.

Cure for epilepsy

The Romans were aware of epilepsy (a condition that affects the brain and causes seizures), though they called it different names. Their treatments varied even more wildly . . .

Cure 1: In 46CE, famous Roman doctor Scribonius Largus wrote a book of medical cures, including a shocking solution for epilepsy. He advised patients

to catch a torpedo fish – a type of electric ray found in the Mediterranean Sea – and give themselves electric shocks!

Cure 2: Understandably, electrocution by fish wasn't that popular (or effective). But there was another, even more gruesome option: drinking the blood or eating the liver of a gladiator!

The reasoning was that many ancient Romans thought blood was the body's life force, and that drinking it would help them stay young and healthy. After a gladiator was killed during a contest, there was sometimes a scramble as bloodthirsty crowd members closed in. Some believed that the fresher the blood, the better – GROSS!

WOULD YOU RATHER

pour sickly-sweet syrup on your dinner

OR a stinky, fishy sauce?

ROMAN DINNERTIME COULD BE FILLED WITH SOME SERIOUSLY BIZARRE DISHES (SEE PAGE 28). BUT THE ROMANS DIDN'T STOP AT JUST THE FOOD – THEY NEEDED SAUCE! THERE WERE A FEW CHOICES, DEPENDING ON IF YOU HAD A SWEET TOOTH, OR FANCIED SOMETHING A LITTLE FISHIER . . .

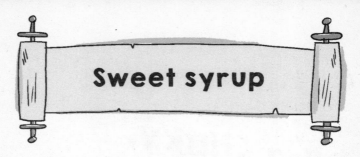

Sweet syrup

Do you have an incurable sweet tooth? Would you always say yes to a pudding? Bad luck. There was no sugar (at least as we know it) in ancient Rome. But don't despair! The resourceful Romans had other ways of sweetening their food. If they needed just a little light sweetness, they tended to use flower petals. When a stronger, sweeter taste was needed, they'd go for honey or grape juice.

Wine or fresh grapes would be boiled down for hours in big pans over fires to create a sweet liquid called *caroenum*. If they were boiled for even longer, they made a sticky, sickly-sweet syrup called *passum*. This was used to sweeten breads and other dishes.

Passum was so sweet it could make your teeth itch! Yet, some Romans drank it without mixing anything in to dilute it. Others mixed it with vinegar and poured it over fish dishes as a kind of sweet and sour sauce.

At least my teeth don't itch any more!

Fish sauce

So, you'd rather take the savoury option? What excellent taste you have! Well, according to the ancient Romans . . .

The Romans didn't have ketchup or mustard to make their food taste nicer. Instead, their number one saucy smash hit was a type of very fishy sauce called *garum*. Pretty much everyone in ancient Rome seemed to love it, and they splashed it on lots of their food. Take one cookbook written by an ancient Roman called Apicius – three quarters of his 465 recipes included *garum* as an ingredient. Yum! But how was this super sauce made, you ask? Let's find out . . .

FISHERS WOULD BRING THEIR CATCH BACK TO SHORE, GUT THE FISH AND CLEAN THEM OUT.

RATHER THAN THROWING AWAY THE GUTS AND OTHER UNWANTED BITS OF FISH, THEY'D COLLECT THEM UP AND PILE THEM INTO BARRELS OR STONE VATS WITH LOTS OF SALT OR SALTY WATER, KNOWN AS BRINE.

THEY'D PUT A HEAVY WEIGHT, SUCH AS A ROCK, ON TOP OF THE GUTS TO PRESS THEM DOWN. THEN THE WHOLE CABOODLE WOULD BE LEFT IN THE SUN FOR ANYWHERE BETWEEN AROUND TWO MONTHS AND A YEAR.

Have you ever smelled fish guts that have been left out in the hot sun for months at a time? Try to avoid it! The fermenting guts would have produced stinky gases, causing the vats to bubble and fizz. Some coastal parts of Italy, Portugal and Spain had giant *garum* factories, with dozens of bubbling, rotting vats filling the air with a serious pong.

Once it had brewed, the lumpy, stinky fish sauce may have been strained and diluted with water to make a weaker mixture. This might have been poured over pork, ladled over lamb and even added to wine. Yuck! Romans made of sterner stuff preferred using the full-strength, undiluted *garum*.

Some Romans even claimed that *garum* was a medicine that could cure a wide range of health problems, including stomach ulcers and dog bites!

So, what will you be sprinkling on your Roman dinner? To remind yourself of some other Roman foods, head back to page 28!

WOULD YOU RATHER

be a priestess in charge of a temple

OR a Roman wife in charge of a household?

LIFE FOR ROMAN WOMEN WAS DEFINITELY NOT AS EASY AS IT WAS FOR MEN. THEY WERE NOT EVEN CONSIDERED ROMAN CITIZENS, AND THEIR MAIN JOB (ACCORDING TO ROMAN MEN AT LEAST) WAS HAVING CHILDREN. BUT, THERE WERE A FEW ROMAN WOMEN WHO TOOK A DIFFERENT CAREER PATH . . .

Priestess

Religion was a pretty big deal in ancient Rome. There were gods galore (see page 38), who were worshipped in temples scattered all over the empire. Temples were managed by priests or priestesses.

Some of the most powerful priestesses were the Vestal Virgins, who were in charge of the temple of Vesta, in Rome. Vesta was the goddess of the fireplace – and these priestesses had a pretty fiery job. One of their duties was looking after a sacred fire that burned in the temple, all day and all night. At least they wouldn't have been cold!

The Vestal Virgins had a pretty sweet deal, compared to many Roman women. They were respected, free from the control of male relatives, and had great job security – unless they did something truly terrible, they would do their work for around 30 years. That's a lot of firewood. Once their stint had come to an end, they'd get to retire with a generous pension. Result!

Roman wife

Ahh, home sweet Rome. Time to put your feet up, maybe make a snack . . . oh, wait – you're in charge of the house, no time to hang about!

Though they didn't have much power in the rest of society, the home was one place where ancient Roman women did have influence. They often held the keys to the house – handy for locking out anyone they didn't want to talk to . . .

Women in wealthier households would have been in charge of supervising the cooking, managing servants, looking after children and generally keeping things running smoothly. Lower class

Roman women might have been servants, or had a job like making clothes.

Sadly, there's not nearly as much in Roman historical records about women as men – most Roman historians and writers simply weren't that interested in womens' lives, and largely left them out. Rude.

Fancy reading about an impressive female warrior who took on the Roman army? Head to page 122 . . .

ROMAN EXTRAS
Getting dressed

Forget jeans and T-shirts – Roman wardrobes were a very different business!

Toga

The ICONIC Roman garment. The toga was worn by wealthy Roman men, and was wrapped around the body like a big sheet. Quite an itchy sheet, in fact – togas were woollen, and would likely have been very hot and uncomfortable!

Tunic

This was the basic item of clothing for most men and women in ancient Rome. It looked a bit like a sleeveless shirt and

could be worn loose or with
a belt. Children would usually wear
mini versions of adult clothes.

Underwear

The big question – did the Romans wear
pants? They did indeed, though not the
sort you might recognise. The average
ancient Roman would wear a loincloth
wrapped around their bottom (bad luck
if yours was made of itchy, scratchy wool).

There are even some mosaics showing
ancient Romans in skimpy garments,
a bit like modern bikinis!

WOULD YOU RATHER

fight against fearsome Boudicca

OR cunning Caractacus?

WHEN THE ROMANS TOOK OVER ENGLAND, THEY WERE SMART ENOUGH TO KNOW THAT THEY COULDN'T RULE THE PLACE THEMSELVES. INSTEAD, THEY FORMED RELATIONSHIPS WITH ENGLISH LEADERS MILD-MANNERED ENOUGH TO MANAGE DIFFERENT AREAS IN RETURN FOR TRADE AND MILITARY SUPPORT. BUT, THE ANCIENT ROMANS DID MAKE SOME ENEMIES ALONG THE WAY, SOME OF WHOM WERE FEARLESS LEADERS WHO PUT UP QUITE A FIGHT!

Boudicca

Are you raring to go on a Roman road trip to Great Britain? Think a battle with Boudicca sounds easy-peasy? Well, don't be quite so confident – make sure you've packed your lucky helmet . . .

Boudicca was queen of the Iceni tribe, from East Anglia in eastern England. Her husband, Prasutagus, was an ally of Rome – but, when he died, the Romans decided to take the territory for themselves. In 60CE, they marched in, stripped Boudicca of her kingdom and wealth, and gave her a whipping to boot.

Boudicca was understandably furious and sought revenge. She joined up with some other tribes and went on an anti-Roman rampage. They destroyed the Roman capital of Camulodunum (now Colchester), burned Londinium (London) to the ground and ransacked Verulamium (St Albans). Was this a *tiiiiny* bit of an overreaction? Possibly. Boudicca's troops managed to kill thousands of civilians on their way who were simply minding their own business.

Despite Boudicca's fierce efforts, the Romans rallied and swiftly defeated Boudicca and her army. The warrior queen died shortly afterwards, maybe from illness or injury, or by taking her own life. But, whether you think she was a rebel hero or made some frankly unwise choices, her memory still lives on today!

Caractacus

Do you think you could act to attack Caractacus? Say that five times fast!

Caractacus was the leader of an English tribe from just north of the river Thames. When the Romans invaded in 43CE, he was NOT impressed, and went to war.

Things did not go well for him, though. After a series of defeats, Caractacus fled north to Yorkshire seeking protection from the Brigantes, another tribe of Britons

ruled by Queen Cartimandua. But, this double-crossing queen gave him to the Romans in return for payment, the rotter.

Caractacus was put in chains and paraded to Rome for execution. But, it turned out that Caractacus was better at giving speeches than battling. He pleaded with Emperor Claudius to spare his life, and was set free!

Cartimandua's schemes were nothing compared to some Roman rulers. Head to page 68 to find out more . . .

Bloomin' betraying Brigantes!

ROMAN EXTRAS
Gladiators galore!

Romans had some gruesome ways of entertaining themselves. A favourite day out was going to a big arena to watch two gladiators battle to the death. Let's go and check out the line-up!

Gladiatrix

OPPONENTS: OTHER *GLADIATRICES*, WILD ANIMALS

MAIN WEAPON: SWORD OR DAGGER

Most Roman gladiators were men, but there was the odd female fighter, called a *gladiatrix*. These fights were rare – women were usually seen as belonging in the home.

Bestiarius

OPPONENTS: WILD ANIMALS

MAIN WEAPON: NOTHING. GOOD LUCK!

Marching out into an arena must have been terrifying at the best of times – imagine doing it without any protection! Some gladiators, called *bestiarii*, were sent to fight animals practically naked, with no weapons at all. The chances of surviving were slim.

Retiarius

OPPONENTS: OTHER GLADIATORS

MAIN WEAPON: TRIDENT

A *retiarius* would be armed with a forked spear called a trident. If they were lucky, they'd also get a dagger, shoulder guard and a large net, called a *rete*.

If they aimed this net right, they could tangle up their opponent so they couldn't fight back.

Murmillo

OPPONENTS: OTHER GLADIATORS

MAIN WEAPON: SWORD

If you were a strong and muscly gladiator, you could fight as a *murmillo*. These gladiators had heavy armour, and moved around *veeerrryy* slowly.

This did have its perks – though there was no chance of them running away from their opponent's blows, they were less likely to be injured by them.

WOULD YOU RATHER

spend all day inventing curses

OR doing laundry?

THE ROMAN JOB MARKET WASN'T LIKE IT IS TODAY. THERE WERE NO VACANCIES FOR LEISURE CENTRE MANAGERS, SOCIAL MEDIA INFLUENCERS OR PROFESSIONAL FOOTBALLERS. MANY ROMANS TOOK WHATEVER JOBS THEIR SKILLS AND BACKGROUND ALLOWED. THERE WERE CERTAINLY A FEW ODD OPTIONS ...

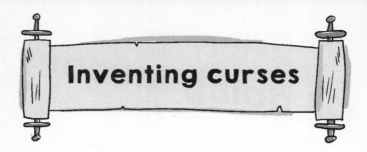

Inventing curses

Are you an expert wordsmith? Think you're great at coming up with top-notch insults? Roman curse-makers were paid by their customers to do just this!

To make a curse, they would fashion a tablet out of a thin, rolled sheet of metal, then scratch or etch it with a message. These tablets normally asked the gods to do something awful to another Roman, like filling their head with maggots, having their eyes struck out by demons, or their heart, liver and buttocks destroyed. Once completed, the curse tablets might be placed close to the intended victim, or nailed to a temple wall.

Unfortunately, curse-makers' tablets were made of lead, which the Romans weren't aware was toxic – so this job could have caused lead poisoning and an early death. Curses!

Writing rude and nasty messages might have been fun at the start, but it likely got pretty depressing after a few years. And, you'd mostly be dealing with seething customers wanting revenge. Probably not the most relaxing of jobs!

Bonus fact

In one hoard of 130 curse tablets found in England, the most common reason for people being cursed was stealing other people's clothes whilst they took a dip in the Roman baths!

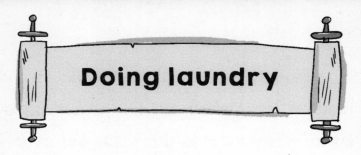

Doing laundry

Mmmm, that delicious smell of fresh laundry, drying in a gentle summer breeze . . . Hold up a second – there's a different smell on the wind, and it's definitely not fresh or fragrant.

Romans in towns and cities didn't wash their own clothes. They'd wait until the dirt and sweat built up to MAXIMUM levels of stinkiness before getting their clothes cleaned. This would happen at laundries called *fullonica*, where cleaners (called *fullones*) worked.

Fullones cleaned the clothes by placing them in wooden vats of water, plus a special ingredient – wee!* Supply was

*Not a completely ridiculous idea. Wee contains ammonia, which is a reasonably good clothes cleaner.

a problem though, as *fullones* couldn't make enough of it to do all their washing by themselves. So, some left large jars out on street corners for people to relieve themselves into. You wouldn't want to bump into any *fullones* with a full jar!

Head back to page 80 for some more Roman jobs!

How it all ended

Nothing lasts forever, and that includes mighty empires.

As it entered its fourth and fifth centuries, the Roman Empire was getting weaker and weaker. In 370CE, the capital was moved eastwards from Rome to Constantinople (now called Istanbul, in Turkey). Twenty-five years later, the empire was split into two halves: east and west.

The western empire's borders started shrinking as lots of different peoples sought revenge on Rome's many land-grabbing missions, and grabbed their lands back for themselves.

In 410CE, the Visigoths, a group from central Europe, decided that they fancied a city-break and invaded Rome. The cheek of it! Vandals (a different group, from what is now Poland) did the same thing 45 years later.

By now, the western empire was weak and feeble and in 476CE, the last western Roman emperor, Romulus Augustulus, was overthrown by invading tribes. This is usually what historians refer to as the fall of the Roman Empire.

But, hold up – it wasn't quite the end. The eastern Roman Empire (known as the Byzantine Empire) with its centre in Constantinople would last for almost a thousand years more!

Glossary

Britons – a people who lived in what is now Great Britain, in Roman times.

Byzantine Empire – an empire born out of the Roman Empire, with Constantinopole as its capital city.

Colosseum – a huge arena in Rome.

Emperor – a ruler of the Roman Empire.

Foricae – a Roman public toilet.

Forum – an open public area in ancient Rome.

Garum – a type of fish sauce.

Gladiator – a trained fighter who fought in battles for Romans' entertainment.

Gladiatrix – a female gladiator.

Gladius – a type of ancient Roman sword.

Legionary – a foot soldier in the Roman army.

Litterator – a Roman teacher, for example of languages or mathematics.

Lectica – a couch or litter used to carry a wealthy Roman around the streets.

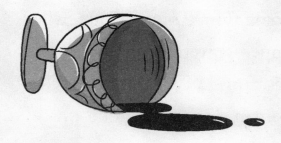

Mosaic – a piece of art made out of small pieces of pottery or glass.

Passum – a type of sweet Roman sauce.

Picts – an ancient people who lived in what is now Scotland.

Pilum – a type of pointed javelin used in ancient Rome.

Praegustator – someone employed by an emperor to test their food for poison.

Roman Republic – an era of ancient Rome from 509–27BCE, where the state was ruled by democracy.

Roman Empire – an era of ancient Rome from 27BCE–476CE, when emperors were in charge.

Scutum – a type of ancient Roman shield.

Sesterce – a type of ancient Roman coin.

Tersorium – a communal sponge left in Roman public toilets for people to wipe their bottoms with.

Toga – a Roman garment for wealthy men made from a long piece of draped cloth.

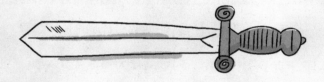

Trireme – a type of Roman ship based on a Greek design.

Visigoths – an ancient people who lived in what is now France, Germany and Spain.

About the author

Clive Gifford's first ever school trip was to see the ruins of a Roman villa, and he's always had a soft spot for the mighty Roman Empire ever since. He has visited ancient Roman ruins all over Europe, from Hadrian's Wall to the El Jem amphitheatre in Tunisia. Clive has written more than 200 books for children and adults, and has won the Royal Society, SLA and Blue Peter book awards. He lives in Manchester, UK.

About the illustrator

As a young boy, Tim Wesson was
constantly doodling, finding any excuse
to put pen to paper. Since turning his
much loved pastime into his profession,
Tim has achieved great success in the
world of children's publishing, having
illustrated and authored books across
a variety of formats. He takes great
delight in turning the world on its
head and inviting children to go
on the adventure with him.

Explore the rest of the series for more fascinating facts and hilarious WOULD YOU RATHER questions!